DUSTY, RESCUE PLANE

adapted by Bill Scollon
illustrated by the Disney Storybook Art Team

White Plains, New York • Montréal, Québec • Bath, United Kingdom

DISK 5

①

Dusty Crophopper, the winner of the Wings Around The Globe Rally, quickly became the world's most popular racer. Known for pushing himself to the max, he won race after race. "Racing is my life!" he liked to say.

But one day, on a training flight, Dusty ran into trouble. His engine stalled, and he fell into a spin! Luckily, Dusty got the engine restarted, and managed to land safely.

Dottie, Propwash Junction's mechanic, told Dusty his gearbox was failing. "If you push yourself, you'll crash," she said. And, it couldn't be fixed. The parts were out of production.

Dottie put a warning light on her friend's dashboard. "You need to slow down," she said.

Dusty was stunned. "So I can't race anymore?"

"I'm sorry," Dottie replied.

That night, Dusty went flying again. Suddenly, Dottie's warning light flashed red! Distracted, Dusty landed hard and skidded into a fuel pump.

"Fire!" Dusty screamed.

Mayday, the airport's only firefighter, tried to put out the flames. But his leaky old equipment was no match for the inferno. There was only one thing to do.

"Pull!" yelled Mayday. Everyone worked together to topple the water tower. A huge wave of water smothered the flames.

The next day, safety officials closed the airport. It would remain closed until Mayday's equipment was updated and a second firefighter was added. That meant the biggest event of the year—the Corn Festival—might have to be canceled.

"We need to get Propwash reopened," Dusty told Mayday. "What if I became our second firefighter?"

The old fire truck was grateful. Dusty was soon on his way to Piston Peak National Park's Air Attack Base for training.

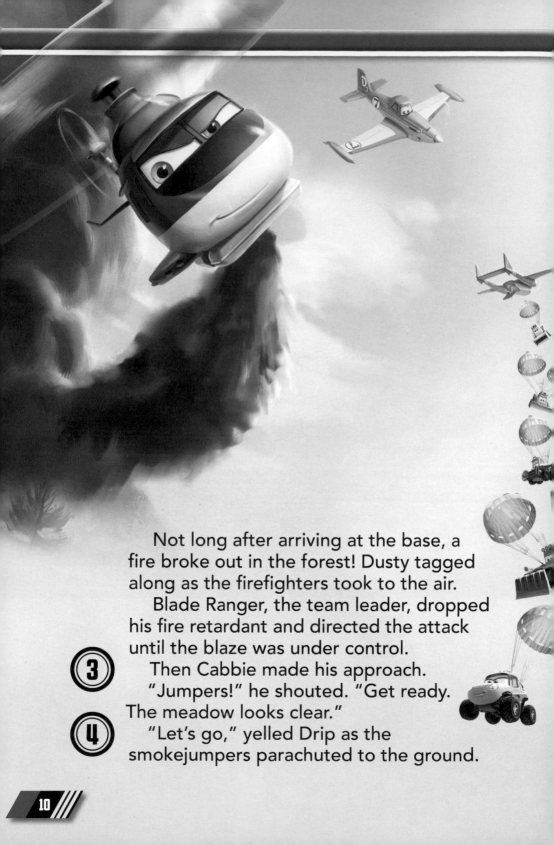

Not long after arriving at the base, a fire broke out in the forest! Dusty tagged along as the firefighters took to the air.

Blade Ranger, the team leader, dropped his fire retardant and directed the attack until the blaze was under control.

3 Then Cabbie made his approach.

"Jumpers!" he shouted. "Get ready. The meadow looks clear."

4 "Let's go," yelled Drip as the smokejumpers parachuted to the ground.

Dusty couldn't wait to start his training. Back at the base, Maru, the team mechanic, gave him pontoons that would carry fire retardant or water.

Blade tried to teach Dusty how to fill them by skimming across the lake, but Dusty nearly crashed! He had a lot to learn. That night, Dusty talked to his friends on the radio. They'd found him a new gearbox! "We'll have it in a couple days," said Dottie.

"That's the best news!" shouted Dusty. He'd race again after all.

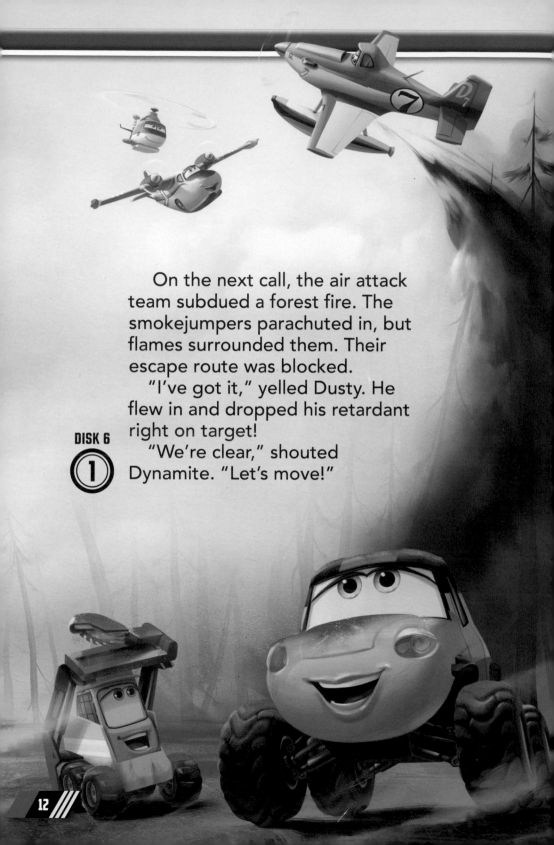

On the next call, the air attack team subdued a forest fire. The smokejumpers parachuted in, but flames surrounded them. Their escape route was blocked.

"I've got it," yelled Dusty. He flew in and dropped his retardant right on target!

DISK 6

①

"We're clear," shouted Dynamite. "Let's move!"

Days later, Dusty got another call from Propwash Junction. The gearbox had arrived—but it was the wrong one. Dusty was heartbroken.

②On the next fire call, Dusty was careless and dropped his fire retardant at the wrong time. Blade was furious!

Dusty tried to refill his pontoons but stalled out and drifted toward a waterfall.

"Restart your engine!" shouted Blade. "Push it!"

But it was too late. Dusty went over the waterfall!

At the last moment, Blade snagged Dusty
with his hoist and swung him to the shore.
But the fire was closing in fast. Blade led the
way to an old mine where they could hide
from the fire.

Dusty told Blade about his damaged
gearbox. "I'm never going to race again,"
he said. Dusty wasn't sure he could be a
firefighter, either.

"If you give up today, think of all the lives
you won't save tomorrow," said Blade.

Just then, the inferno swept past the
mine. Blade moved to protect Dusty from
the flames.

When the fire passed, Dusty and Blade found a clearing and took off. But Blade, badly damaged by the heat, crashed to the ground!

3 Dusty radioed for Windlifter to carry Blade back to the base. There, Maru got right to work. "The surface burns are bad," the mechanic said. "But the interior damage is repairable."

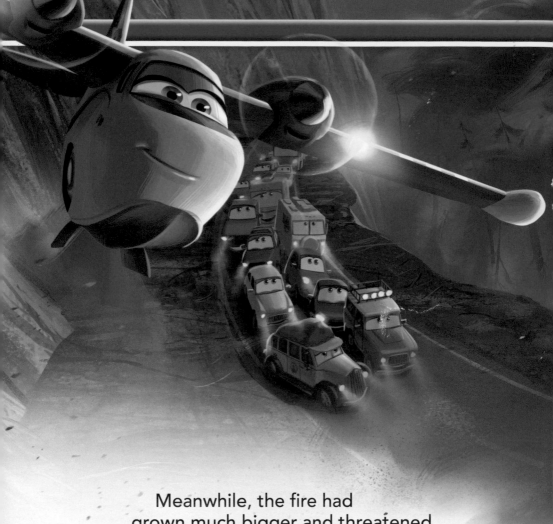

Meanwhile, the fire had grown much bigger and threatened the park guests as they tried to escape. The air attack team flew to the rescue—straight through the fire!

"It's the fastest way to the main road," Dipper explained. "Hold on, Dusty!"

Smoke and hot embers swirled around them until the planes broke through to clear skies. Then, one by one, they dropped their fire retardant.

Dusty lined up and made the final drop.
The fire was out! The guests were saved!
"Great job, Dusty!" shouted Dipper.

But two more guests were trapped
on a bridge. Dusty raced across the
park to help them. He flew straight
up the face of a waterfall and filled
his pontoons. The red warning light
flashed, but Dusty didn't slow down.

With his tanks full of water, Dusty
put out the fire, and the guests
hurried to safety.

Just then, his gearbox broke down
and Dusty crashed into the forest!

It was days later when Dusty finally came to.

Maru said he had managed to fix all the crash damage. But there was more. Maru had also made Dusty a new gearbox!

Blade had more good news. Dusty had shown the bravery and skill needed to be a certified firefighter.

"You earned it," he said. "Now spin 'er up!"

Dusty smiled as his engine roared to life!

Dusty raced back to Propwash Junction. Now that Mayday was completely refurbished, the airport had two certified firefighters. Dusty and Mayday were both proud of their shiny, red paint jobs.

And the safety officials reopened Propwash just in time for the Corn Festival!